Magic Charms: The Adventure Begins

by LOUISE MARIE MILLER

This book is dedicated to my fourth grade teacher,

Miss Nicole Markes.

CONTENTS

Chapter One

A New Home

Kasandra Cortez was moving all the way to America from her home in Brazil. As she walked out the front door of her house, she saw her mom and dad packing up the car.

"Why do we have to move again?" Kasandra asked her parents, as she pulled her suitcase out to the car and laid it in the trunk.

Dad replied, "We are moving because America has better schools and jobs."

Before he could finish, Mom added, "Remember how things have been hard for us ever since Dad lost his job last summer?"

"Yes," Kasandra said, remembering how hard it was for her parents to make payments to avoid being evicted from their house since late May. Dad struggled to make enough money to pay the bills, and Mom counted every penny when she bought groceries each week.

"Dad thinks he can get a better job if we move to America," Mom said smiling down at her.

1

"Hey you might like it there," said an unexpected voice from behind Kasandra. It was her eighteen year old sister, Maria. "Hey relax, it's only me Kitty."

Maria called Kasandra Kitty for short; it was part of the secret sister codes they liked to make up together.

"You scared me!" Kasandra said as she ran over to Maria.

Maria's long, silky, black hair was blowing in the mid-August wind. She was wearing a blue dress with flowers on that Maria and Kasandra had made together. She had sneakers on, and Kasandra thought it was an odd fashion choice. But Maria made it look good. Maria made *EVERYTHING* look good.

"Hop on in girls!" Dad called as his tie was blowing in the wind, just like Maria's hair.

The girls skipped on over to the car and got in without a word. Maria was smiling. Mom smiled back. The girls understood that Mom welcomed this adventure. She loved to try new things. For example, Mom called Thursday night dinners, 'Try It Thursdays.' The family had tasted different recipes ranging from Ghost Pepper Fajitas to Cranberry Chili on such nights.

Mom had blond hair, unlike Dad, Maria, and Kasandra. Mom also loved the colors green, blue, and yellow. Mom loved these because they were the colors of the Brazilian flag. *She is going to need some new favorite colors once we get to America,* Kasandra thought to herself as Mom was reviewing with them how to say certain words and phrases in English.

Mom had been working hard to get the family ready for this big change of culture and language. Mom even started to cook 'American foods,' like Philly cheesesteaks and banana pancakes. Kasandra thought the pancakes were actually pretty good.

Soon they arrived at the airport. "Our flight is in twenty-seven minutes. Does anyone have to use the bathroom?" Mom asked, as she gestured to the left.

"Sure, Mom. I need to fix my makeup quickly," said Maria, following Mom in the direction of the ladies room.

"Kasandra, do you have to go?" Mom asked.

"No thanks, Mom. I went when we were at our house," Kasandra said quickly.

"Okay," replied Mom, as she and Maria walked away.

"Come on over here, Kasandra. Take a seat," Dad said to his youngest daughter.

"Okay," Kasandra replied and walked over to Dad. She was biting her lower lip, something she always did when she was nervous.

"Is there something you want to tell me honey?" Dad asked politely.

"Yes, Dad..." Kasandra started, "I am scared!" she said, bursting into tears.

"Relax! Are you that scared honey?" asked Dad.

Kasandra nodded. "I am scared because I am worried about starting at a new school, and moving to a new house, and speaking a language I hardly know. Plus I won't be with my friends," Kasandra said, her voice trembling.

"Oh baby girl... don't you cry! I know things will be tough, but we'll manage. You will make new friends, and have a room that you don't have to share with Maria. And you don't have to worry about speaking another language. We have it all sorted out. You will have private lessons on speaking English. Your new school will only be a half mile from our new house, and you can even walk to school on warm days," Dad said, as he lifted her up and spun her around in his arms.

"*Eu te amo,*" Kasandra said, now smiling.

"I love you too," said Dad, sitting down now and giving her a kiss on the cheek.

Mom and Maria returned with about ten minutes to spare until it was time for their flight to take off. "Well, we better get going. My watch says it is twelve-fifty. We still have ten minutes, but to get good seats we need to get there early," said Mom, looking much more relaxed.

They approached the counter at their departing gate.

"*Ola!*" said the woman at the counter.

"*Ola,*" said Mom and Dad, handing her the flight tickets.

"We have a one o'clock flight to America," said Dad, as he gave the woman the flight slip that they received when they first arrived at the airport.

"Esta tudo bem," said the woman, opening the door to a long hallway that led to the passenger entrance to the plane.

Before they took their seats Mom asked, "Do you and Maria want to sit together?"

"Yes," said Kasandra, her eyes widening. She loved sitting with Maria. They played games like bicycle and tic-tac-toe. Sometimes Maria even let her use her headphones!

Maria and Kasandra sat down together when they heard an announcement overhead: "Please be seated. We will start our trip to the United States of America. We will start flying in about three minutes."

Maria was listening to music on her headphones. After a few minutes, she turned to Kasandra and said, "Hey cutie, look out the window."

They were flying. Higher. And higher. Until finally, they were soaring in the air. Kasandra looked down and saw her old home, and how beautiful it was from up in the clouds. It was amazing!

About two hours later, Kasandra felt she was getting bored, so she took out her doll and made her dance as if she was a princess. She wanted Maria to play with her, but did not want to interrupt her sister's peace. Almost an hour later, Maria reached for something in her bag. The item she pulled out was wrapped in what looked to be some sort of green, blue, and yellow material. No wait. It was a Brazilian flag! Maria handed the colorful package to Kasandra.

"Here," Maria said, smiling at her little sister. "From one Cortez to another," she said, setting the flag down on Kasandra's lap.

"Do I open it now?" asked Kasandra.

"Whenever you want Kitty," she replied, still smiling. Kasandra opened the package as carefully as she could. She did not want to rip the flag of her home country. Inside was a dress. It was no ordinary dress though. Maria had made it. It was blue, green, and yellow with white stripes.

"*Eu amo isso!*" exclaimed Kasandra, hugging her older sister.

"I knew you would love it!" said Maria, now smiling too. "I also have paper dolls, and some coloring books too. Do you want to color?" Maria asked, showing Kasandra all of the different books.

"Yes please!" said Kasandra picking up one of the books and a pack of 'Kids Fun' crayons. Then it felt like time was flying just like the airplane did through the cotton candy clouds that dotted the sky.

Chapter Two

Connecticut, USA

As the plane approached American ground, Maria and Kasandra cleaned up the supplies and coloring books they had been using and put them in their backpacks. They had to hurry because Mom said the plane would touch down in about five to ten minutes. It was a six hour flight and their backs were killing them.

After they landed on American soil, the family slowly walked out of the crowded plane and started over to where they would get a rental car. The walk was worth it. Kasandra thought it felt good to stretch her legs.

They soon got the rental car, and drove from New York all the way to Connecticut. They traveled past many plains and cities, before seeing a sign for 'Hartford,' and finally arriving at a grand looking colonial house. It had navy blue shutters resting against light blue siding. Kasandra immediately loved it, and so did Mom, Dad and Maria.

Remembering the dress that Maria gave her on the plane made Kasandra think about how it was special because it was something Maria had made in Brazil. She wondered if Maria would make things in America different from what she had made in Brazil.

Now Kasandra stood outside looking up at the house. It was a two-story colonial with four bedrooms, two bathrooms, and a large kitchen and backyard. Mom had told her that the house had an attic too.

"Girls, go on in. It's unlocked. You can pick which rooms you want. Then start unpacking your stuff. All the rooms have closets," Mom shouted from the car.

They two girls smiled at each other and skipped up to the front door. They walked through a hallway and directly into the kitchen. It was huge, almost two times as big as the one at their house in Brazil! Then there was the living room. It felt so homey to Kasandra. There was a stone fireplace and hardwood floors. *The table Dad handmade last year for Mom for Christmas would go great in the living room,* thought Kasandra, as she her eyes scanned the shiny, clean room.

Kasandra was awakened from her daydream when Maria burst into the living room and said, "I found the bedrooms, they're upstairs. I didn't go in 'cause I thought you would want to see them too. So you could, you know, pick which room you want."

"I'm coming," said Kasandra, running over to her older sister. They went up the stairs which were covered in carpet. The second floor of the house seemed kind of odd to Kasandra. There were two hallways, separated by a giant open room between them. Kasandra said, "You there, little girl…. What hall do you choose? Door A, or Door B?"

Maria giggled and replied, "I pick… hall A. You have to start at the beginning, right?"

"Oh Maria, you and your ways," said Kasandra, laughing harder than before. "Let's go then."

Maria stopped Kasandra, then shouted, "Last one to the first door is a rotten egg!"

Maria started running. What else was Kasandra supposed to do? So she ran too. They began running down the long hall until they reached the first door. They ran into the room and fell on top of a mattress that Dad had brought in a few minutes earlier.

"I think it was a tie," panted Maria, not wanting to admit she lost to a girl six years younger than her.

"You know I won," said Kasandra, giggling.

"I know," Maria admitted.

For the next ten minutes the girls stayed in this room giggling, and racing each other from wall to wall. Finally Kasandra said, "Do you want to check out the next room?"

"Sure," replied Maria, her eyes widening.

They ran to the next room and it was almost as big as the first. Kasandra loved it. It was a large, open space with an enormous closet situated at the center of one wall. If she told Maria she liked it, would Maria let her have it? Maria was a 'growing girl' as Mom called her, so she must need more space of her own.

"Hey, Maria, can I ask you something?" said Kasandra, feeling the surge of confidence to ask her question.

"Yep, I'm here for ya, sis," she said calmly to Kasandra.

"So... I was wondering if I could have this room. I really like it. And I thought if I chose this room, you could have the other because you're a 'growing girl' like Mom says. So..." Kasandra hesitated, "could I please have this room?" She stared down at the shining hardwood floors beneath her feet.

"Sure," said Maria gazing down at the floor like Kasandra.

"What? Did you just say that? I thought you would want this room!" exclaimed Kasandra, not knowing what to do next.

"It's all yours. But first, can I take a look at the other rooms?" asked Maria.

"Well, let's think... sure!"

They went to the other bedroom, but it was not as amazing as the one they had visited just before. It did not compare to the second room they saw either. But the last one was Maria's favorite. It had a built-in desk and a bay window.

The girls walked down the second hallway. There was a bathroom (that was huge!), as well as Mom and Dad's new bedroom.

It was almost two times as big as Maria's, and that was much bigger than the guest room. At the end of the second hallway was a door.

"Do you think we should go in?" asked Kasandra, sounding excited.

"Sure lil' sis," said Maria, shining her perfect smile. The whole family said she had Mom's smile. Kasandra thought so too.

They opened the door and went in. It appeared to be an empty cupboard with a staircase leading upward. The staircase was circular. The two girls walked up its winding path. Once they reached the top, they saw a small circular room with nothing in it except them. There were cobwebs all over and it was dark. Maria picked up her phone and turned on her flashlight.

"Gee, thanks," said Kasandra happily.

They searched everywhere for clues to tell them where they were. Then Maria said, "Kitty, this must be the attic! Mom and Dad were talking about it on the plane! I heard them!"

Kasandra started hopping around. "Ohh! That makes sense! We should make this our secret hideout. We can come up here to make plans when we play spies, and do puzzles and games, and so much more!"

"Cool. And we don't tell anyone about it, understand?" asked Maria.

"Yes ma'am," said Kasandra with her best French accent.

Then they heard something. It was Mom! That probably meant it was time to eat their sandwiches and then go to bed. After all, it was nine-thirty at night. So the sisters headed down the winding stairs, through the hallway, and down the carpet-covered stairs, and into the kitchen.

Kasandra was starting to think that maybe life in America wouldn't be so bad after all.

Chapter Three

The Room Do-overs

Kasandra woke up on the mattress that was lying on the floor in her new room. She knew today was going to be a good day. She was going to decorate her room today!

She quickly got up and put on her robe. She soon ran down the stairs to get breakfast. Dad had gone to the grocery store last night when they first arrived in America. Mom was down in the kitchen with Maria. Maria always woke up just on time like Mom. Kasandra always slept in and was always tired.

Mom turned and spoke to both girls. She said "So the one bummer about your father's new job is that he will go to work before you go to school. So he'll start tomorrow morning, and you will start in a few weeks at your new school."

Ugh… school, thought Kasandra. That was her number one worry. What if she got picked on? What if she spaces out in front of the whole class? What if her teacher is really mean? But, instead of complaining, she simply replied "Okay" just like Maria had.

Mom was making bacon and eggs, a traditional 'English Food' with a Brazilian twist. It was the girls' favorite breakfast food. While her mom cooked, Kasandra looked around the family's new kitchen. She noticed that all of the boxes for her room were sitting next to Mom's table. It was not a big table, but it was full of love. It was the table that Dad had made for Mom for Christmas last year. It was Mom's favorite gift ever. Maria and Kasandra loved it just as much as Mom did.

Kasandra turned her attention to her mother. "Hey, Mom. Can we start the room do-overs today?"

Mom replied instantly, "Yes! Of course! What are we going to do with all of this stuff down here?"

"Can I start?" asked Kasandra, ready to jump out of her chair. The granite countertops were her favorite part of the kitchen. The marble floor came in a close second.

Kasandra picked up her first box and ran up the stairs. The warm fuzzy carpet was comfortable under her bare feet. Kasandra turned into the 'Bedroom Quarters,' as she and Maria had decided to call this part of the house. She went to the first door to the right, and into her room. It was white, but Mom and Dad found paint that the previous owners had left there. *So why not paint my new room? It was painted before,* thought Kasandra. So she went back down the fuzzy, warm carpeted stairs and into the kitchen.

"Where is Dad?" she asked, smiling at her mother.

"He is down in the basement. And if he's not there he is in the garage. That is just to the left of the basement," Mom said clearly enough for Kasandra to hear the directions she gave. Kasandra had never gone down to the basement before. *Well, there is a first for everything,* she thought as she went through the dining room. A grand wooden table had been left behind by the old owners, so Mom kept it. It looked great next to Mom's French dishware in the clear glass-paneled cabinets. The table was covered with Mom's white tablecloth that complimented the blue shade of the dining room.

The door to the basement was in the area where you first enter the dining room. Kasandra thought it looked a lot like a hidden door. Just like the attic. Its dark wood looked great against the smooth blue paint on the walls. Kasandra opened the door and crept down the stairs. It was bright, and there were numerous lights on the ceiling. *It looks like Dad was hanging stuff up in what is going to be our 'everything room,'* Kasandra thought as she looked around for Dad.

"He must be in the garage," she mumbled to herself.

Kasandra followed Mom's instructions and turned left. There it was. The door to the garage was also wood and stood out against the soft blue paint. It was just like the door to the basement. She went inside. The garage was a large, open space, and Dad was in the far corner setting up Mom's rocking chairs to put on the front porch. They had to take them apart so they wouldn't break on the way to America. The family had their valuables shipped to America by boat.

Kasandra ran over to her dad and gave him a hug. "Dad, ya think I could use some of that paint you and Mom found?"

"Why?" he asked Kasandra.

"I sort of…. want to paint my room," said Kasandra, looking up at her father.

"Okay. Just be careful," Dad warned her.

"I will!" she said as she stomped over to the paint. "What color should I do?" Kasandra quietly asked herself. There were pails of blue, pink, purple, light blue, green, turquoise, and black paint. She decided on the turquoise. It would look good on her walls. She grabbed the paint, and ran upstairs.

Kasandra skipped up the fuzzy steps and into her new room. She had set up her desk the previous night before going to bed. On top of it was a paintbrush and some other personal items. Kasandra quickly got to work painting. *This could take hours,* she complained in her head.

Suddenly, Kasandra heard something. She turned around to see that it was only Maria dragging her boxes up the carpeted stairs.

Kasandra went back to painting. Dad didn't know, but she snuck up the pink and purple cans of paint too. She had planned to do a fun swirly design using the different colors. It would be great! All of her new friends would love it! The rest of the family would like it too.

After a little while of painting, Mom told the girls that she had finished setting up her room and asked them if they needed any help with their own rooms. Maria accepted Mom's offer, but Kasandra said she wanted her room to be a surprise. She continued painting the walls, and then moved on to her swirly design. She was almost finished when she heard a knock on her door. It was Maria.

"Come in," called Kasandra as she kept painting.

"What's…."

Kasandra didn't let Maria finish, "I'm painting my room!"

"I finished my room," said Maria, as she picked up a paintbrush off Kassandra's desk. Then Maria picked up a container of turquoise paint, and worked on the swirly design alongside her younger sister.

When the painting was finished, the two girls set the mattress on top of the bed frame Dad had assembled for her earlier. Dad had brought it up to Kasandra's new bedroom when she was downstairs eating her breakfast. The sisters did not notice him then because Dad went out from the garage, around the side of the house, and in through the front door, before going up the stairs. Next, they put up the shelves and Kassandra's dresser.

The girls had to go out to the car to gather more of their belongings. So they ran down the stairs and out the front door. They saw the car parked in the driveway which led to the garage. They went down to the car. Inside the trunk, were seventeen boxes. They found the ones marked 'Kasandra,' and then ran back and forth to bring the boxes into the house. Mom yelled at them for running in the house a few times too.

The two girls put the last of the boxes down and fell onto the bed. Inside the boxes were things like books, dolls, toys, sheets, pillows, and clothes. They set up the books on the bookshelf, and put Kassandra's clothes into her dresser. They also made the bed, which turned into an epic pillow fight. Kasandra won, and both girls held their sides with laughter. After several minutes of giggling, Maria said, "Hey, I have to go to the bathroom," and she walked out the door.

"Okay," said Kasandra, as she started putting more craft supplies on her desk. Maria snuck up behind Kasandra and scared her!

"Ahhhh!" screamed Kasandra, using her quick reflexes to hit Maria with a pillow.

"Ouch!" exclaimed Maria, beginning to laugh again.

The two girls soon went downstairs for lunch. As they ate their sandwiches, Mom said, "Girls, some of the neighbors are coming over on Sunday, a few weeks before you start school."

Ugh, school again, thought Kasandra as she ate her PB& J in silence. Kasandra enjoyed her mother's sandwiches, especially the ones she made on the weekends. They had extra love in them (and maybe some extra peanut butter too!).

"Hey, you want to go finish your room do-over?" asked Maria, motioning Kasandra up the stairs.

"Sure."

Kasandra ran up the stairs with her older sister.

Chapter Four

Party Time!

It was late August and the Cortez family had been in America for a few short weeks. Kasandra awoke in her bed and realized it was Sunday. *The neighbors will be over at twelve o'clock noon. We still have a few hours to prepare,* thought Kasandra, yawning. She enjoyed the view from her window. It felt so big and open, almost as nice as the view she had from her bay window in Brazil.

In America, Kasandra was slowly becoming more accepting of what people in her country called *'O novo mundo.'* In America, that meant 'the new world.' She was beginning to feel more comfortable expressing her personal ideas and feelings each day that she awoke in this new land.

Kasandra arose and ran through the hallway and down the stairs. The carpet felt warm and fuzzy against her bare feet. She saw Dad in the living room, and saw that he was hanging something up over the fireplace. It was a flag. But, it was no ordinary flag. It was an American flag.

"Dad," she started, "Why?" Just seeing her family start to participate in this new culture, and doing new things made Kasandra feel sad. It was hard moving and calling this new place home. She felt like running away from her own father. But she stayed put.

"Sweetie, this is for the party only. I would never want to make you feel bad, especially in a new country. You know that," he said to Kasandra wisely.

"I'm sorry, Dad. I just thought..." she didn't even finish. She just couldn't. And she wouldn't. She just didn't.

"Come over here. We need to talk... now," he said, almost sounding sorry for putting up the flag. Kasandra walked slowly over to her father. "Okay. Listen. I know this is hard for you. Can I tell you something? I don't really want to do this whole move to America thing either. But, there are better jobs here for me and Mom, and better schools for you and your sister. I promise I will take down that flag after the party. Pinky promise?" he asked her, offering up his little finger.

"Okay, pinky promise," she said, locking pinky fingers with her dad and giving them a firm shake.

Kasandra walked into the dining room hoping to find Mom. But she wasn't there. Kasandra checked in the basement, in the garage, and in the spare bedroom. She looked in Mom and Dad's room. There she was. Mom was lying on the bed. She looked tired, very tired. Kassandra went over to her mother. Mom said, "Honey, I didn't sleep well last night. So we're only inviting one family over. There last name is Morrison. They will be over around four o'clock."

"Okay. Do they have any kids?" asked Kasandra.

"Yes, in fact, they do. They have a ten year old daughter that is in your grade. Maybe you could be friends. They also have an eighteen year old son, only two years older than your sister. I think they might get along together." Mom winked at Kasandra. Then they burst out with laughter.

When they quieted again Mom said, "Honey, I am going to get back to my morning Sudoku puzzle. Now be a doll and tell your sister to cook breakfast today."

"Okay," replied Kasandra. *I wonder if I will be friends with this girl in my grade. Who knows? Maybe Maria will like this new boy. Or old boy in our case.* Kasandra smiled to herself and skipped down the stairs to the kitchen.

After breakfast, Kasandra couldn't stop bugging Maria about this new boy. It seemed so clear to Kasandra: Maria would like this new boy and Kasandra would have her first friend in America.

The morning quickly turned into afternoon, and as four o'clock neared the girls put on their party dresses. These were also outfits that Maria had made in Brazil three years ago. The dress that Kasandra selected to wear tonight was given to her from Maria on her ninth birthday. It was her favorite present of them all!

Now Kasandra was ten (almost eleven), and she was supposed to be more mature. Or in other words, more like Maria. But she wasn't thirteen yet, so she would continue to be (and act like) a child. She thought it was fair. So it was. Fairer than fair. Even more fair than fair could be. At least Kasandra thought so. But everyone else.....well, Kasandra didn't know. Dad was fun to play around with, and Mom was a good-feeling, happy kind of person. So Kasandra thought her family was perfect. And it was. In some ways at least.

Kasandra went up to the bathroom to pull her hair into a bun. While she was smoothing out a few loose strands of hair, she heard the doorbell ring. *Here they come,* she thought, as she stepped on the stool to look out the window. The Morrisons had an expensive looking car.

Maria walked over to the bathroom door and said to Kasandra, "Get down here. Mom wants you to welcome our guests."

"Okay," replied Kasandra, as she quickly slipped on her shoes.

This will get interesting, Kasandra thought, somewhat hoping that Maria would like this new boy. Kasandra always wanted to go to a wedding. She had to remind herself that nothing happens that fast. First, what she had to do was get them together. But how?

Before she could think about it anymore, Kasandra was downstairs waiting and watching as her mother and father opened the front door. The first thing Kasandra saw was a sea of blue. The whole family was wearing blue: Blue shirts, blue pants, blue shoes, blue bows, and blue dresses. The family seemed to enjoy being such a sight. But the boy, he wasn't smiling like the rest of his family. He did not seem to be enjoying it at all. At all. He seemed embarrassed. Really embarrassed.

Kasandra settled her eyes on a tall woman, the mother of the family. She had black wavy hair. Kasandra thought she saw a streak of blue in it. *Of course, more blue.* The man had a dimple on his left cheek and had freckles all over his face. His hair was red with what seemed like a tint of blue. *Was that even possible?* He also had round glasses that looked like the ones she imagined Harry Potter wore in the books.

Yep, Mom had made Kasandra read books in English. Mom always said it was to 'increase their vocabulary.' Maria thought it was not necessary because she had studied English since January of last year when they first learned that they would be moving to America. Kasandra however, thought reading was amazing! She would read in any language, even if she didn't know the language! She loved it.

Looking again at the family, Kasandra noted that the son had red hair and freckles just like his father. He had no tints of blue or streaks of blue in his hair. It was just normal. Kasandra saw Maria smiling at him. *Oooh! She likes him!* thought Kasandra as she looked at her older sister.

Next, Kasandra looked down at the young girl who appeared to be about the same age as her. She had blond hair and rosy cheeks. Her hair was curly and also had a streak of blue in it. She was wearing a dress. A blue dress of course. She had blue heels that made noise with every step she took. Kasandra thought it was annoying. Very annoying. But she held her breath for a long moment and decided it was best to just deal with it.

Before long, Kasandra found that she was actually having fun with this new family. Well, only when they were eating pizza. After they ate, Mom asked Kasandra to show the young girl her bedroom. Kasandra agreed, but only so her mother wouldn't look bad in front of the neighbors. Kasandra didn't enjoy it very much, but did it for Mom. Anyways, no one wanted Mom to be angry, not even Dad.

One time back in Brazil, Kasandra was playing kick the can with her old friends and the can went flying and hit the family car. Mom pulled Kasandra inside, and sent her to her bedroom. Of course all of her friends went home after that. Kasandra definitely did not want to make her mom angry today!

When Kasandra and the girl with the curly hair went up to Kasandra's room, the first thing the girl said was, "Tacky."

Kasandra felt a surge of anger. She wanted to cry. Instead, Kasandra politely asked the girl what her name was. The girl walked around Kasandra's room, touching items one-by-one on Kassandra's bookshelf.

After what felt like forever, the stranger finally replied, "My name is Jessica Morrison. Unlike you, I have been in America all my life."

Kasandra stared silently at her, stunned by how rude this Jessica was to her.

Jessica continued, "Are you going to MaryEllen Bay Middle School?"

Kasandra replied quickly, "Yeah, I was hoping we could b-"

Jessica cut her off mid-sentence with a loud sigh and said, "Oh. Okay. Just asking." She seemed upset that Kasandra was going to the same school as her. In fact, she was upset.

Kasandra was guessing that Jessica was popular in school and probably filthy rich. *Yeah, filthy is probably the right word to describe her,* thought Kasandra, as she fixed her bed from where Jessica had been sitting on it.

After a long, awkward silence, Kasandra asked Jessica if she wanted to go back downstairs for chocolate lava cake. Of course Jessica said yes, not even knowing that Kasandra's mom made the best chocolate lava cake ever.

When the Morrisons left at ten o'clock, Kasandra was tired. Too tired to even put on her pajamas. She plopped down on her bed and was out cold within seconds.

Chapter Five

School

Kasandra woke up and noticed that something was different. It was three days after the Morrisons had visited, and it was Kasandra's first day at MaryEllen Bay Middle School. She was excited, but nervous at the same time.

Kasandra got dressed in her 'first day of school outfit.' She wore a plaid shirt, black skirt and red Vans sneakers. Mom said the red shoes looked good with her curly black hair. Maria and Dad thought so too.

Kasandra walked down the hall and into Maria's room. Kasandra saw Maria was wearing her first day of school outfit too. She was sharpening her pencils to put in her new leather pencil box. Maria was wearing a turquoise dress that had pink flowers going from the bottom up to her midsection. She had a black belt around her waist, and a bow too. Maria looked stunning. Everyone thought so. Everyone. Maria's long silky hair seemed to be even silkier today. She wore it up in a ponytail with the bow positioned in the center.

While Kasandra was wondering if she would ever be as pretty as her sister, Maria spoke, "Hey Kitty, you want me to sharpen your new pencils too? Mom got them personalized to say 'Kasandra Cortez.' Between you and me, I think Mom had a lot of fun at the school supply store."

"Me too," said Kasandra, as she looked at her pencils. Her name was written in pink, and the pencils were white with paint splatters covering them. The splatters were blue (which was now Kasandra's least favorite color), purple, yellow, red, orange, and green. Kasandra loved them. Kasandra also had a new pencil sharpener, eraser, white board marker, crayons, and a small pack of tissues. She had pink and white erasers. She also had a pink leather pencil box with a zipper and everything. Her folder was pink with a swirly design on the front, and if you made a rubbing with your fingers on top of it, you could feel the texture. Of course, Kasandra's notebooks matched her folder too. She had five notebooks; one for homeroom, one for history, one for math, one for writing, and one for whatever else may come along the way. Each notebook was pink. She also had a binder that matched her folders and notebooks. It was like a dream come true!

Kasandra took her things and ran downstairs to put them in her backpack. Her new backpack was also pink with a tint of purple on the front pocket. Clearly, Kasandra's favorite color was pink. Everything she loved was pink. All pink. Except her family. Obviously.

She walked down to the kitchen and saw her mother making pancakes. Mom always put milk chocolate, peanut butter, and semi-sweet chocolate chips inside her pancakes. As Kasandra and Maria were eating breakfast they realized Dad had already left for work.

Mom told the girls that their classes for learning English will be on Thursdays. Mom said the teacher seems very nice, and that her name is Ms. Colelli. She had taught at MaryEllen Bay Middle School for six months, so she was pretty new to the school. And so was Kasandra. She thought it was great to have a teacher who was almost there as long (or as short) as her.

Mom also told Kasandra and Maria that she would drive them to school today, only because she didn't start her new job until next Monday. Mom was going to be a speech therapist at an elementary school only twenty minutes away from home. That meant she would be working at MaryEllen Bay Elementary School, only five minutes away from the middle school.

After breakfast, Mom called to the girls to hop into the car to head to school. It wasn't a long drive. When they reached the school, Mom gave Maria and Kasandra each a kiss on the cheek, and they were off! Mom smiled as she drove back toward their house.

Kasandra was walking down the hallway of her new school when she bumped into someone. All of her books went flying onto the floor. It took her a moment to figure out who was in front of her. It was a girl with straight blond hair. She looked to be the same age as Kasandra, and seemed to be heading in the same direction. She wore a lavender colored dress and turquoise high heels. Her hair was up in a ponytail with a braid in the center of it. There was something different about the girl. Kasandra guessed by the red-tipped cane she carried that the girl was blind. She seemed and looked like she could see, but Kasandra thought that maybe she really could not.

"I am so, so, sorry!" apologized Kasandra, as she looked up at the girl.

"It's all right! Let me introduce myself. I am Darling Adams. And you are?" she said suspiciously.

"Oh! I am Kasandra Cortez. I just moved here this August. Do you know where history class is?" replied Kasandra.

Darling spoke up at once, "Yes, I do know where history is. I am actually heading there now. Come along with me."

The girls walked down the long hallway together, talking about school and other stuff they did that summer. Then Kasandra got up the courage to ask Darling, "So, you are blind?"

"Why, yes, I am. Is that a problem? Are you here to call me mean names too?" she replied shortly.

"No! Of course not! Who would call you mean names anyway? You are a person with feelings just like everyone else!" blurted Kasandra, as if she was going mad.

"Some people just don't think people with disabilities are as cool as they are. For instance, Jessica Morrison. Have you met her yet?" said Darling calmly.

Kasandra thought for a moment, and remembered the Morrisons who had been to her house only three days earlier. "Yes, I have. She seems like a spoiled brat."

"Don't say that!" said Darling quietly.

"Why not?" replied Kasandra quickly.

Then, Darling replied even faster, "Because her Mom is the principal here!"

"What?" said Kasandra, her mouth dropping.

"Let's go. First period is about to start!" said Darling.

The instant friends rushed side by side to their first period class.

Chapter Six

Shakira in History

When the two girls arrived at their history class they walked over to the wall where the rest of the students were standing. The teacher's name was Mrs. Giamoni. She was tall and had dirty blonde hair. She was wearing a dress with large round buttons and a thick belt. She sat down at her desk, after writing on the chalkboard, 'Today we will start with a pop quiz.' Kasandra thought that her handwriting was rather dainty.

Kasandra took a seat, opened her book, and turned to page three hundred and ninety-four, just like the teacher had asked. Mrs. Giamoni passed out papers, and Kasandra looked at the questions written on the page in front of her. They were all about Brazil.

1. What is the capital of Brazil?

Kasandra wrote as quickly as possible. She scribbled down, *Brasilia*. All of the questions she knew, even one about the most popular food in Brazil!

After the pop quiz, the class checked their answers together in small groups. Kasandra was in a group with Darling and another girl she did not know. She had vivid red hair and lots of freckles. She wore contacts lenses, unlike anyone else in her grade.

Darling had told Kasandra that the girl in their group was named Shakira. Shakira was also one of Darling's friends. She seemed nice, but she seemed to worry too much about how she looked. She explained to Kasandra and Darling that she was afraid all of her super popular friends would laugh at her if she wore her glasses to school. They were purple and had pink and yellow stripes on the frames. But unlike the other kids in her grade who wore glasses, Shakira was the only one with an open lens on the bottom. She explained that people would call her names like *'Disco Grandma'* and *'Party Pooper.'* Kasandra automatically felt bad for Shakira. She wasn't selfish and mean like Jessica. She certainly did not deserve to be called names.

The trio decided to meet later that night. Kasandra volunteered her house for their meeting place because she knew she had that perfect little room at the end of the hallway where they could gather. Only Kasandra and Maria knew about it though. Was it too much of a risk?

Kasandra thought she could trust her new friends. They seemed really nice. She felt like she could welcome them to her house anytime.

Later that day after school, Kasandra was lying across her bed reading her English book, *Cinderella*, when she heard the doorbell ring. *Yes!* she thought as she skipped through the hall. She went past Maria's room, and Maria stuck her head out the door.

"Whatcha doin'?" Maria asked, her face only peeking out of the door. She was at her desk, and was doing something that looked like homework.

"I am heading downstairs to see if my friends are here yet," replied Kasandra as she tried to get past her sister, who was now standing in the hall.

"Okay, just don't interrupt me. I am going to call Matthew."

"Who's Matthew?" asked Kasandra as she snuck past her sister.

"The super cute boy who is our new neighbor," said Maria, walking back to her room.

"Yes!" shouted Kasandra.

"What?" said Maria turning back around to look at her little sister. She looked startled. Very startled.

"Nothing," said Kasandra, running down the stairs. She was still wearing her outfit from school, but her hair was down now.

She walked to the bottom of the stairs and the doorbell rang again. Kasandra quickly opened the door and looked at the figure standing there. It was Darling.

"Hey. I was told by my dad that Shakira will be here in half an hour."

"Okay. Do you want to come in?" said Kasandra, greeting her friend with a hug.

"Sure," replied Darling, looking around even though she could not see.

The two girls ran up the stairs, almost getting yelled at by Mom. Once the girls were safe in Kasandra's room, they started to talk. Of course Kasandra had to mention the room hidden at the end of the east hallway.

Suddenly, Darling said, "Can I see it?"

Obviously Kasandra said yes, so the girls headed towards the end of the hallway. The door was wooden, and Darling felt her way into the room. Kasandra thought it was so amazing that someone could learn all about their surroundings by using other senses than just sight.

The girls went into the circular room. In the room, they opened up Kasandra's jewelry box. Inside were four rings, all a different color; pink, blue, purple, and yellow. Kasandra said she wished that one of the rings was plaid, and then she would wear it every day! She was just joking of course.

The girls continued to laugh, and soon after that Shakira arrived. Kasandra and Darling brought Shakira to the hidden room and showed her the rings. They each decided that they would take a ring, and wear it to school every day. Kasandra took the purple one, Darling took the blue one, and Shakira took the pink one.

The girls kept the promise they had made to one another to wear their rings every day for the next two weeks at school. While wearing her ring, Kasandra noticed that strange things started to happen whenever she walked through the hallways at school. Kasandra observed that when she walked past papers hanging on the wall, the papers would shake, and eventually fall off to the floor.

Mrs. Giamoni noticed that Kasandra looked out of sorts. She asked her if she was okay, and of course Kasandra said she was. She didn't want anyone to worry about her. Or worse... be suspicious of her.

During lunch one afternoon, Darling and Shakira said that strange things were happening to them too. The girls decided that Darling and Shakira should come over to Kasandra's house again right after school. They needed to talk about it. Immediately.

Kasandra told her friends that she had an English lesson during recess, so they couldn't talk then. It was Kasandra's first lesson, and her first time meeting her new tutor, Padma Colelli.

Professor Colelli, as Kasandra was told to call her, wore a peacock print t-shirt with a black sweater. She had her long, curly dark hair up in a ponytail and she wore black flats on her feet. Kasandra thought this could turn out well for the pair. Professor Colelli was very nice and shared with Kasandra that she believed strongly in stopping bullies from picking on others. Kasandra liked that.

Since moving to America, Kasandra learned how to read unfamiliar words, like nugatory, oaf, mite, and idyll. Some of these words made Kasandra giggle. She wondered if there was a word other than 'perfect' to describe something just as divine. (For those of you who don't know what divine means, it means 'simply delightful' or 'happy.') If Kasandra knew the word divine, someone had to come up with something that meant 'perfect.'

At the end of the school day, the three girls walked home together. Kasandra was excited that her new friends were coming over to her house again. They decided they would meet in the tiny cupboard at the end of the east hallway. It was a quiet place for them to 'hang out,' which really meant for them to talk about all the strange stuff that had been going on around them in school. They thought there might be a connection between the odd events.

Time flew by as the girls chatted, yet there was still so much more for them to discuss. They made a plan to meet each other once again on Saturday, only two days away.

Later that night, after Darling and Shakira went home, Kasandra felt that something odd was going to happen. Something very odd indeed.

Chapter Seven

At The Park

At the park later that weekend, the girls wrote notes and played games together. They wrote down things they noticed about one another; what they like, and other unique qualities they saw in each other. This made them feel more confident and comfortable around one another.

John, one of the boys in the girls' enrichment, history, math, and science classes, was at the park too. He couldn't turn away from the girls. He thought Kasandra was cute. In fact, John liked her. He had liked her ever since she arrived in America, though he just didn't have the courage to tell her. Kasandra didn't know John that well, so they barely talked to each other.

John couldn't help but notice the strange things that had been happening to the girls in school. He wanted to help. But how could he? *Why would they even want my help? They are so perfect. I'm probably over-thinking the situation,* John thought this to himself as he watched the three girls giggle and play, and take occasional notes about one another.

Kasandra, Darling, and Shakira continued their games until they heard a cry. It was not a sad cry, but it was a scared cry. They ran over to one of the largest oak trees in the park. There were two small children, a four year old girl and boy, standing under the tree looking up at the branches. They appeared to be twins, and they had very sad looks on their faces, as if they were about to burst into tears.

Darling ran as fast as she could over to the twins and said, "Jeremiah, Julia? What are you two doing over here without Mum and Dad?"

Darling must have recognized the pair by the sound of their cries, thought Kasandra.

"Please don't tell them we left! The cat ran out the door, so we ran after it. Now Lucy is stuck in that tree!" said Julia, pointing up at the top branch.

"How could Lucy get up there?" demanded Darling, scolding the two children.

"We think she was scared because a bird was sitting on our bedroom window. And she jumped out onto the roof, climbed down, and ran across the street..." started Jeremiah, who was quickly cut off by Darling.

"You ran across the street?" Darling questioned.

"Yes, but it was for Lucy," pleaded Julia.

"Can you please get her down?" asked Jeremiah, as he looked up at Darling admiringly.

"I can't right now. I am wearing my heels, not sneakers. I would do it kiddos, but I am not wearing appropriate shoes for tree climbing. All we need is a miracle that Lucy comes down without getting hurt, or worse, falling." Darling sounded as if she felt very sorry for her younger siblings.

The three girls turned to one another, feeling awful for the twins. Shakira, who had known Darling since kindergarten, was wearing dress flats. Then Shakira turned her attention to Kasandra in amazement. Kasandra was wearing sneakers!

The twins stopped crying and looked up at the strange new girl. Kasandra looked down at her feet in amazement too.

"Well, would ya look at that?" said Shakira, starting to smirk.

Kasandra hesitated, then replied, "Fine. I'll get Lucy for you. I might not be the best climber, but I made the Portuguese Gymnastics team twice. But it was only for the school, not like I was in the Olympics or anything like that." Kasandra let out a nervous giggle.

Looking up at the stranded cat, Kasandra started climbing. Up, and Up, and… Up. She was almost there when she heard a creaking sound. *Crack*. *Oh no!* thought Kasandra as she continued her climb towards the top, only faster now. Kasandra felt the warmth of the mossy oak tree as she quickly crept up its solid trunk. She was so close to Lucy, she could feel it. Finally, she saw Lucy. Lucy was right in front of her. Kasandra quickly reached out for Lucy, and the cat went to her gracefully.

When the two were about ten feet off the ground, Kasandra realized that her ring was stuck five branches above them. Kasandra allowed Lucy to climb down the last few feet herself, and then Kasandra went back up to retrieve the ring on her own.

When Kasandra finally reached the branch where her ring sat, she grabbed the ring, and began her descent. She was ten feet from the solid ground when she heard another *Crack! Not now. Please not now. Please, please, please, with extra sugar on top. Please don't fall. Keep your balance, Kasandra! Don't Fall.* Kasandra swiftly felt her way around the broken branch. She made it! At least halfway. She still had another five feet to go. Kasandra was as careful as a mouse, and as quick as a cheetah. She was amazing.

Meanwhile, John was watching Kasandra's brave act. He thought she was incredible. And she was. While he was watching, he heard another *Crack!* from the great old oak. Kasandra looked down and watched the branch under her fall down onto the ground. Quickly, Darling moved Julia and Jeremiah out of the way before the branch made its landing right where they had been standing. Kasandra, however, was falling from the oak tree.

Chapter Eight

John Finds a Way to Help

After Kasandra's fall, the others gathered around Kasandra, looking at her. More like *staring* at her. Before she fell from the tree, she had managed to get Lucy down safely. After the fall, Kasandra was surprisingly unharmed. Everyone thought it was a miracle that she didn't even have a scratch on her body!

Kasandra blinked. She looked up at the world around her. She saw that she was lying on the towel that the girls had been using when taking their notes. But why? After Kasandra fell, the others, including John, who had ran over to see what all the commotion was about, brought her over to the towel to let her rest.

The friends worried that Kasandra was in a coma. A coma is a state in which you are alive and well, but your brain has stopped functioning, and you cannot wake up. In other words, Kasandra could not wake up. She would not wake. At least not for a while.

Now Kasandra was awake and well again, remembering everything that had happened in the tree. She just had to ask one question though. So she asked the crowd of friends around her, "What happened after I fell from the tree?"

"You fell... well, you didn't fall. You were hovering just about two feet off the ground. Then, you slowly started coming down onto the grass," said Shakira, trying to sound smart.

"Er. What?" Kasandra was stunned.

"That's what happened!

"What?" Kasandra asked again. She felt confused and in wonder at the same time.

Then, John scurried up to the front of the crowd. He said something like, "Hey is there a spot you girls hang out at? Ya know, in private? 'Cause that might be where we want to talk about what happened today."

"Oh. Okay. You can come eat in the hall with us tomorrow. I'm going to use my 'eat in the hall' pass. Meet us in the hallway near the cubbies five minutes before lunch starts. We get our lunch first, ya know," replied Kasandra, looking dreamily into John's eyes.

"Don't worry. I'll be there," said John, his face bright red with embarrassment.

John quickly scurried away. It's not every day that you meet the girl of your dreams and get invited to eat lunch with her!

Darling, Kasandra, and Shakira, with the twins in tow, walked home feeling more than ready for a good night's rest.   Once Kasandra got home, she ran into her sister's room without being yelled at by Mom. Mom got curious when the girls, or anyone, ran in the house.

Kasandra almost knocked over a vase once, but luckily Maria caught it. Yep she's in the girl's baseball league at high school. She would have one more year of school before college. She was in the eleventh grade, and was very excited about that.

Kasandra and Maria were having their first 'sister sleepover' in the new house. Kasandra arrived home at about seven thirty, and the sisters finished getting settled by eight.

It was a Friday night, so the girls planned to watch a movie before bed. Maria was in her white and blue pajamas and wore a blue night cap. Her silky black hair was in a tight bun on the top of her head. She looked beautiful. As usual.

Kasandra picked the movie *Beauty and the Beast.* It was her all-time favorite movie. Maria loved it too. They hadn't been able to see the movie in a while because they were waiting for Maria to get her own TV. That's right! Maria has a flat screen TV in her bedroom!

As the girls prepared for the night, Kasandra remembered that she had not yet told anyone in her family about falling from a tree, or going into a two and a half hour coma. No one knew. No one other than Darling, Shakira, John and the twins knew about her epic fall.

Kasandra planned on keeping today's events a secret, but was it really worth it? She had no clue. It was odd enough that it actually happened. Kasandra wondered *how* it even happened. It was like a…..
miracle.

Now, it was time for Kasandra and Maria to get their sister sleepover started. Maria pulled out the dusty old pull-out mattress from under the bed. It was an ugly shade of white, only because the family used it for their camping trips. They would put it on the bottom of the tent so it would be like a camping cushion. Or that was what they called it at least. Back in Brazil, the family would camp out on the warm sandy beaches almost twice a month.

Kasandra loved her new house, friends, and school, but life in America was just different. The whole fall-from-a-tree-without-being-harmed thing was a little far-fetched for her.

While watching the movie, Kasandra cuddled as close to Maria as possible. Whenever Kasandra felt down, Maria always made her feel better.

When the movie came to an end and Kasandra was settled in the camp bed, she thought to herself, *Maybe I should stop worrying about the fall. John might know something. Plus he's kinda cute.* After that she fell asleep.

The full moon was looking down on Kasandra. Already asleep, Kasandra did not know of the constellation above the mountains, hanging over the trees. It took the shape of a cat.

At school on Monday, Kasandra used her eat-in-the-hall pass that she had earned. Kasandra thought the idea was perfect. The hall was a nice private place to talk. After all, no one could hear you because of the noise from the cafeteria. John, Darling, and Shakira thought it would be perfect as well. Especially for this occasion.

After getting their lunches from the cubbies outside of their homeroom classroom, they headed down to the 'jungle hallway,' more commonly known as the guidance hallway. The group saw a figure guarding the entrance to the hallway. It was a lunch supervisor. (For those of you who are in school, you would probably know what the scariest thing at school is the *Lunch Supervisor!)*

This particular lunch supervisor looked familiar to Kasandra. She had short brown hair and was wearing a pink shirt, with black sweatpants and pink flats. In her hair she wore a big black bow. She was quite the sight. That was for sure. She looked to be about thirty-five years old. Kasandra always had a knack for accurately guessing that kind of stuff.

Maybe I'm just over worrying, thought Kasandra as she walked slowly down the jungle hallway. Kasandra always loved the jungle hallway. It reminded her of the famous river in Brazil. That river is called the Amazon. (For those of you who don't know what the Amazon is, it is a river in Brazil that is about 4,345 miles long. For those of you who thought it was a website that you can shop online with, you are wrong. They are two totally different things!) The hallway reminded her that when something bad happens, a good thing will follow. The hallway held that meaning only for Kasandra. It was her special spot. When she was there, she only thought about good and happy things.

Today was different. Kasandra felt mysterious. She felt an odd, shivery feeling inside her bones. Something was changing. She just had to find out what.

During lunch, the group of four kept discussing what could have happened at the park. They tried to find answers. But they couldn't figure it out.

Finally, John spoke up, "Maybe during free period we could meet in the library. We can look for books about mythology. I think I saw one on E.T. abductions."

Kasandra glanced at John and said, "I don't think I was abducted by aliens, but the library does sound like a good idea. I say we do it."

"So you're cool with it Kasandra?" asked John.

"Yep," replied Kasandra quickly.

Kasandra was smiling know. Everything was better. Everything.

Chapter Nine

At the Library

It was time for the foursome's free period. During this time, students are free to do any activity that they want. In Kasandra's case, she preferred to go to the library. It was silent there, especially at this time of day. During free period, no one went to the library.

The librarian's name was Miss Soul. She always wore her hair up in a tight bun. Kasandra loved having her even more than her last librarian, Mrs. Jordon. Mrs. Jordon was her favorite teacher in Brazil. In all of Brazil.

Miss Soul wore big round glasses, and she was very tall. She was five foot seven. She was the youngest teacher at the school, after all she was only twenty-three. Maybe that's what Kasandra liked so much about her.

Miss Soul reminded Kasandra of Maria. It wasn't how she looked of course. It was her spunky attitude and love for fashion. Every day she wore tight black dresses and limited edition Dr. Martens. Her favorite pair of Dr. Martens were the 'year of the fire rooster.' Every once in a while a dark brown curl would pop out of Miss Soul's bun and curl right in the middle of her forehead.

When Kasandra walked into the library, Miss Soul popped up from behind her messy desk. She had so many books on her desk you wouldn't know there was even a desk there!

Miss Soul walked over to them with at least seven big books in her arms. Then she said, "Kasandra darling! No offense, Darling."

"None taken," replied Darling as she turned away from the adventure books.

"The *Beauty and the Beast* book is ready for you." continued Miss Soul.

Kasandra quickly replied, "Can I pick it up after we leave? We are actually looking for books on *Mythology*. Do you know where I can find them?"

Miss Soul always had a quick answer about the topic of any kind of book. She said, "Yes, I do know where they are. I am a librarian after all. They are in the last aisle to the right. Also, they are next to the books on constellations."

"Thanks," replied Shakira, who was ushering Kasandra away from the librarian.

As the four students went through the books on Mythology, they saw, *Mythology and Your Spirit Animals, Mythology: in the Constellations,* and *Susie Learns about Mythology.* None of the books sounded fit for them.

Then, they heard a buzz. It startled everyone. Finally, Shakira said, "Geez, it was just my phone guys! Ooh! A new *Instagram* post from NASA!"

"What does it say?" asked Darling, who had popped up out of nowhere.

Kasandra could see out of the corner of her eye that Darling was holding a book called, *How to Control your Anger with Younger Siblings.*

Shakira replied, "It says, '*Someone by the name of Janet Parkinson, one of our fellow scientists, saw a pattern in the sky last night at precisely ten o'clock PM. This is believed to be a new constellation. It was in the shape of a cat. It will be decided today at noon to either become a new constellation or just a drawing in the night sky. We will keep you posted!*'"

"Isn't that cool?" asked Shakira, after she finished reading the paragraph.

"Yeah," said the others, getting bored with the 'space talk.' However, once Kasandra heard about the constellation, she had an idea. She thought to herself for a moment. *Why would I fall from a tree, and my favorite animal is a new constellation? Maybe I should check out that spirit animal book. Maybe even that book on constellations too.*

Kasandra wondered if her new team would help her figure out this mystery. What could be happening? Kasandra had no idea. It would be good to have the help of her friends, because she didn't know what challenges may be ahead of her.

So Kasandra took the two books over to the table where the others were seated. The library tables were circular, and had lots of books piled on top of them. Those books were there not only to read, but to keep you hidden if you needed to read something privately. It was kind of like a wall to protect you.

The chairs around each table were not too big, but not too small. They were all sorts of colors; red, yellow, blue, violet, green, you name it. It was very colorful coming from a teacher who loved the color black!

Kasandra always loved the high ceilings. They made it feel so open and airy. There were at least one-hundred shelves in the library.

She sat down with the rest of her friends and opened up *Mythology and Your Spirit Animals*. She had learned so far that some strange things happen when your spirit animal starts to emerge. Strange things can happen to your physical being and to your health. Or in Kasandra's case, falling from a tree.

She had figured out one more thing, that spirit animals can show themselves though *nature*. This meant that the constellation that was discovered last night could be her spirit animal! That made so much more sense! Just, would anyone believe her?

Kasandra started second guessing herself about her discoveries. Was she really correct about the things she had found out? Once again, she had no clue. As usual. It still didn't make complete sense. Why would she feel like attacking people when she got mad?

A few weeks earlier, Kasandra overheard Jessica making fun of Darling's blindness. Kasandra felt like physically attacking her. Specifically, she felt the urge to scratch out her eyes and feed them to the crows. They would enjoy them. Then, she thought to herself it was wrong and just walked away.

Kasandra was different now. She wondered what her life would be like if she still lived in Brazil. Would her spirit animal emerge there too? Or was it just in her new home? Or was it because of her new friends? Or her new school? Was it only going to happen in America?

Kasandra had so many questions. But only one was answered so far. She knew that her friends felt this way too. Even John. They all felt like their emotions were heightened making them want to physically attack others who are doing someone wrong.

Darling had also heard Jessica talking about her disabilities. Shakira was with Darling, but she felt as if she could just talk it out with Jessica. Darling on the other hand, wanted to ram into Jessica, even if she would later regret her actions.

A few days ago, John felt like scraping his brother with large claws like those of a parrot. It was pretty scary.

It was hard for the group of four to understand these new feelings. Yet, they had no idea they could end up risking their lives. They all had a spirit animal *inside* them, and it was ready to come out.

As the group was quietly talking, Darling asked, "So we all have a spirit animal ready to emerge? But what about the other kids our age? Do our parents have a..."

"We are the only ones with this animal spirit thingy," interrupted Shakira.

"If and when these things do emerge we have to be able to control them. And keep them a secret," said John and Kasandra at the same time.

Kasandra and John smiled at each other. Darling and Shakira both let out an "Oooh!" to mock the pair. The group thought it was hilarious!

Kasandra started, "We need to figure out what our spirit animals are. They can be any animal; graceful, mean, ferocious, happy, or dangerous. We need to figure out what they are as soon as possible."

"Okay," said everyone else, snapping back into reality.

Kasandra was taking charge, just as she was supposed to be. As the group departed, Kasandra thought. And thought. And thought. Then the idea came to her. *Nature.* The answer was nature. Nature showed it to her, through the stars. So her spirit animal must be a cat! The other spirit animals must show themselves through nature too.

Kasandra had to tell the others as soon as possible. They already had recess and lunch, and free period was over. After school was her only chance. They could fake sick. No, too dangerous. They could pass notes. Yes, that was it.

Chapter Ten

Busted

During Mrs. Giamoni's history class, Kasandra wrote a note to Shakira. She wrote:

Dear Shakira,
Our spirit animals will come to us through nature. Mine   is
a cat. I know because of the constellation the other   night.
It was right over my house. Please write me back-
K.C.

She slipped it under her desk. Shakira sat right behind Kasandra, so the transition was easy. After a few minutes, Shakira slipped a note under the desks in return. Shakira had such nice handwriting. She wrote back:

Dearest Kasandra,

I will look up more about nature's animals. If I find the right stuff, I can match the characteristics.
P.S. I love science!

Yours, Shakira

Once Kasandra started to write back, a dark shadow fell over her desk.

"Tut, tut. Miss Cortez. Meet me at my desk after class."

It was Mrs. Giamoni. *Great,* thought Kasandra. Mrs. Giamoni returned to her teacher desk, and started grading papers from a few days ago.

Soon enough, the bell rang. Kasandra remained at her desk. Darling and Shakira walked by and asked if she was coming with them to Math. But Kasandra stayed put. Finally, everyone was gone. Kasandra walked up to Mrs. Giamoni's desk.

"Please, sit down," said the teacher, giving Kasandra an evil grin. Kasandra sat in the nearest chair.

"Tut, tut. What were you doing young lady? Because I know for a fact you should have been reading about the Civil War. Were you not?" the teacher continued, her eyes beaming with great pleasure.

Kasandra was twiddling her thumbs, barely paying attention. But, she knew she had to reply. Without lying. Mrs. Giamoni was strict, and she could be mean.

One time Darling got in trouble for talking in the halls, right after Mrs. Giamoni had said that they could talk about the Great Depression.

So, Kasandra replied, "I was writing a note to Shakira Umbridge."

"Tut tut. Well then, let's call her in. Shall we?" asked Mrs. Giamoni, smiling her most evil smile.

Then she picked up the phone, and dialed the number for the school office.

"Hello, I would like to call a student to room 407."

The muffled voice of the office secretary responded, "Who do you wish to call down?"

"I would like to call down *Shakira Rose Umbridge.*" *Wow. Rose?* thought Kasandra, as she listened to Shakira's name being called over the loud speaker.

As Shakira walked into the room, she looked at the teacher and then at Kasandra.

"Miss Umbridge, please take a seat," said the teacher, her eyes widening even more.

Shakira sat down, watching the teacher's twisted face looking down at her.

"Now, was Miss Cortez over here passing notes to you during class?" asked Mrs. Giamoni, staring Shakira down.

Shakira looked over at Kasandra. Kasandra could see she was biting her lip, and her face was turning red. Kasandra quickly mouthed to her, 'It's okay.'

Shakira just nodded, and turned to face the teacher. After a moments silence, Shakira spoke up, "Yes."

Shakira looked at Kasandra, and continued, "Well, no. You see-"

Mrs. Giamoni quickly cut her off. "I've heard enough! You two have probably broken over thirty school rules!" Mrs. Giamoni shouted, "If your fate was up to m-"

Mrs. Giamoni was interrupted by the sound of the door opening. Miss Soul entered the classroom and walked around the desks, seemingly admiring the purple floor tiles.

As she floated around the room, Miss Soul spoke directly to Mrs. Giamoni. "Gabriella, can you tell these girls what thirty school rules they have just broken?"

Mrs. Giamoni was left speechless. She lifted up her finger, as if she were about to say something, but then lowered it.

The librarian came to a stop and said, "If you don't mind, they will come to the library instead of your room, and I will give them jobs to do around the library. We will start today. Since Math period has just begun, they will come to my room. Now."

As she clapped her hands together once, the two girls scurried into the hall. From out in the hallway, Kasandra and Shakira could hear Miss Soul say to the angry teacher, "And before you ask,

Gabriella, I will call Michelle and tell her the girls will not be attending Math class today."

Miss Soul walked out of the classroom with her head held high. Miss Soul was a beautiful, brave, and forceful young *woman.*

As they walked down the hallway, Kasandra couldn't keep her thoughts all bundled up inside her head. After all, Miss Soul did save them from Mrs. Gaimoni's punishments. So, Kasandra blurted, "Thank you so much for that!"

"For what?" asked the librarian, whose face was still looking forward and did not appear to be at all concerned.

"For saving us from Mrs. Giamoni," said Shakira before Kasandra could respond.

"Oh, that? That was nothing," replied Miss Soul, whose smile was as bright as can be.

Once they reached the library, Kasandra and Shakira got straight to work. They had to organize all the books from nonfiction A to nonfiction O. That meant they might get to take a peek at the nature books.

The girls looked at quite a few books to compare characteristics. Kasandra already knew that the cat was her spirit animal.

"Hey, Kasandra? Check this out! I think I found my spirit animal!" said Shakira, who was just three aisles away from Kasandra.

Kasandra dropped her books and ran over to Shakira. Shakira was looking up the characteristics of a deer.

"Mine's a peacock," she said, looking up at Kasandra, her eyes widening.

"Great! Now we just have to find out Darling's and John's," said Kasandra, like it all came down to this one moment in her life.

Shakira frowned at what Kasandra said. It made her feel that her friend doubted her work. So she said to Kasandra, "Actually, I found theirs too. Darling's is a deer, and John's is a parrot. I based it off of their characteristics and special abilities. It was almost easy to do. Especially with those two."

Shakira hesitated, then said "So… do you like John?"

"Shakira!" blurted Kasandra, accidentally hitting Shakira in the back of the head.

"Ouch!" shouted Shakira.

"Sorry about that. And maybe I do like him a little bit," said Kasandra, starting to blush.

She had never told anyone about her crushes before. Mom would tell everyone that her 'adorable little baby is all grown up.' Maria would get nosey. And Dad would punch John in the face. But only if he had to. Dad was not one of those guys who walked around punching people in the face. He wasn't that bad. He was okay.

"Oo!" said Shakira.

"Geez, Shakira, it's nothing to panic about," said Kasandra, her face turning even redder.

So the girls spent all of Math period in the library, organizing books. It was actually kind of fun. The two girls discovered all sorts of books they did not even know existed!

After school the gang walked home together. Kasandra kept the spirit animals secret. She was going to tell them soon. But when? She had a plan. This time.

On the walk home, Kasandra said to her friends, "My Avó is coming over this weekend. My grandfather died before I was born, so my grandmother likes to visit with us, ya know, just in case. So if we want to meet at my house, we need to meet on Sunday afternoon. My grandmother is coming Friday night, and leaving Sunday morning. Precisely twelve o'clock. Is that okay with you guys?"

"Cool with me," said John, as he turned down his driveway.

Shakira, who had known John her whole life, walked into her house next to his after saying, "Okay."

After Darling went home, Kasandra walked down a few more blocks, then entered her own house. Maria was already home. She was sitting at the kitchen counter, working on her homework. Kasandra didn't have any homework, so she went right into the living room, took off her shoes, and put away her belongings.

Kasandra laid down on the couch and started writing her story in her notebook. It was her writing notebook. She wrote all of her ideas and thoughts in there. Shakira had something similar. Just, hers was a *journal*. At school people say, 'Journals are for boys, and dairies are for girls.' To Kasandra, the only difference between a journal and a diary, is that a journal is all about thoughts and feelings. Not about secrets you keep from your friends, like in a dairy.

When she finished her writing, Kasandra heard the dinner bell. That meant supper was ready! Kasandra dashed into the kitchen. They were having macaroni and cheese, a classic American dish. At least that's what mom called it. Eh, the family went with it anyways. The meal was quite enjoyable. Dad liked it so much, he wanted Mom to make it for *his* birthday!

After dinner Kasandra heard talking on the way upstairs to her bedroom. She checked Mom and Dad's room, the bathrooms, her bedroom, and finally Maria's room. That's where it was coming from, Maria's room. She peeked into Maria's bedroom, and saw her laying on the bed talking to someone. It was a muffled voice. It wasn't loud, but it wasn't exactly quiet either. It was the voice of a boy. A young boy. Not like a boy in Kasandra's grade, or a boy as old as Dad. It was a *teenage* boy. Maria never talked about boys before. Or talked to one like this.

As Kasandra got closer to Maria's door, she stepped on something. One of her pencils. She winced in pain. One of her pencils must have fallen out this morning! After hearing Kasandra wince in pain, Maria walked slowly into the hallway. Kasandra quickly ran into her bedroom and hopped under the covers of her warm bed.

A few minutes later, Maria came in to say goodnight. Maria walked right in, and rolled over Kasandra. She shouted, "Steamroll!" and the girls burst into laughter.

After mom yelled at them, they started to settle down. Soon after, Maria questioned Kasandra about listening to her conversation on the phone. "Were you eavesdropping on my conversation on the phone?"

"Okay, you got me. I was just coming in to see if you were going to say goodnight to me. Was it a boy?" asked Kasandra with great wonder.

"Yes it was," said Maria, but she wasn't finished yet. "It was Matthew, and he asked me to the Halloween Dance. What should I say?"

"I say you should go," said Kasandra, daydreaming of Maria's future wedding with Dustin.

"Thanks, Kitty," said Maria, as she walked out of the room and into her own.

Kasandra shivered as her older sister walked out of the room. This happened all of the time now. Whenever Kasandra heard the word 'kitty' or 'cat' she would shiver. Maybe she just wanted to make sure no one knew her big secret.

Shortly thereafter, Kasandra she fell into a deep sleep, and started dreaming about a girl with a normal life.

Chapter Eleven

Avó's Visit

The rest of the school week was just as boring as the past ones, so Kasandra focused on finding out what was going on with her and her friends. She had to find out what their place on Earth was. She knew that *they* meant something. Something special.

Before dismissal from school on Friday, Mom picked Kasandra up at the school an hour early. This was because they were getting Avó off the plane today.

Once they arrived at the airport, Kasandra saw her grandmother for the first time in America. Kasandra ran over and hugged her tight. Dad grabbed his mother's suitcase, and Mom and Maria dashed over to the old woman and hugged her.

When they got home from the packed airport, Mom asked Kasandra to show Avó where she would sleep during her visit. As the pair walked up the long staircase, Kasandra said, "How are you grandmama?"

"Well I'm doing just fine. You aren't. I can tell," said Avó, smiling down on her granddaughter's bright face.

"Oh grandmama, you and your *conhecimento*," replied Kasandra, who was now holding her grandmother's hand.

"Kasandra, honey, all knowledge comes with a price, as long as you are willing to embrace it," replied Avó wisely.

"And by that you mean, 'don't get sick, go to school!' Am I right?" asked Kasandra.

"Well you might be. But, what I'm trying to tell you is that you need to pay attention to your surroundings. To your spirit animal," said her grandmother as she walked into the spare bedroom across the hall from Mom and Dad's room.

Kasandra's mouth dropped. How did Avó know her secret? Did anyone else know? She had to say something. So, Kasandra asked, "How do you know about my spirit animal crisis?"

"I know a thing or two," said Avó unpacking a black leather book. The book looked old and dusty. It was not a pretty sight, that was for sure.

Avó took out the book, and motioned Kasandra to sit down on the bed next to her. Kasandra sat down with the old woman. She noticed there was a lock on the weathered cover. Avó took Kasandra by the hand, and pressed Kasandra's hand against the tattered book cover. Almost immediately when Kasandra's hand touched the cover, the lock popped right off.

Odd, thought Kasandra, as Avó lifted the flat cover of the book. Inside the pages were dyed almost an ugly yellow color. The inky handwriting was old and was slowly fading away.

Then, Avó said to Kasandra, "This book holds all the answers to your troubles child."

Avó handed Kasandra the book and walked out of the room and down to the kitchen. Kasandra remained seated on the bed, reading the diary of someone from years ago. The front page read:

'This book is property of: Loriel Cortez'

That's interesting, thought Kasandra as she flipped through the pages. Then, she remembered something. Last January in Brazil, her grandmother told her about a woman who was named Loriel Cortez. It was like the idea just popped out into the world from her head. Loriel Cortez was her grandmother's grandmother!

Kasandra continued to read.

Dear diary,

Today mother told me something I will never truly understand. I have a spirit animal, and am destined to save the world's animals. My best friend, Julianna, has one too. I'm so curious about what's going on in my life. Will it last forever? Or will it end soon?

Yours, Loriel C.

After reading that clip of the diary, Kasandra closed the book and ran out into the hallway. She quickly ran into her room and hid under her bed covers. She had to read the book in private. So, she continued reading.

Dear Diary,

Today I figured out something new. There are bad guys in the real world. Today, when Julianna and I were fighting a forest fire in Australia, we met someone new. They said they were there to destroy the habitat of the koala. They were brother and sister. They used to work for the animal guard organization, but turned evil because they had a disagreement with the other recruits. Their names are Vulture and Crow. I'll write to you soon,

Loriel C

That was the end of the entry. *So I am a recruit for an organization? And, let me get this right, bad agents started all this commotion? My team, we are the newest recruits!* thought Kasandra, putting her new favorite book down on her bed.

Kasandra ran down the stairs, hearing her mom ring the dinner bell.

"Kasandra, honey, hurry up! We're having ghost pepper fajitas for dinner. They're better off hot!" Kasandra heard Mom yell up to her.

"Coming Mom!" shouted Kasandra.

After eating her delicious ghost pepper fajita, Kasandra looked over at her grandmother. Then, Avó winked at Kasandra. Kasandra gave a confused look back at Avó.

Avó had always wanted her grandchildren to grow up in a safe community. She also always gave the girls clues to learning valuable lessons in life. She claimed that that was what a good grandmother does, protect her grandchildren with everything she had. Everything.

Soon after dessert, Kasandra and Maria had to go to bed. Avó walked up the stairs next to Kasandra. Kasandra couldn't help but ask, "Why did you give me Loriel Cortez's diary?"

"What are you talking about child?" Avó asked, as she turned into her bedroom and closed the door.

Kasandra thought that maybe this was all just a dream. Maybe it was to her. And only her. But no, this was just a day in the real world.

Kasandra lay in bed wondering how her Avó knew her secret, and that maybe there were others like her. Others. That's right. Kasandra wasn't alone. *There must be thousands of agents out there all over the world! Avó must know something about the whole animal guard thing. Is it really true that my great-great- great grandmother was part of the animal guard? She seemed like an adventurous person!*

Kasandra hoped a good night's rest would clear her head from any more nasty thoughts about the animal guard. But, first, Kasandra had to tell the others about the animal guard, and about Crow and Vulture too.

The villains she discovered could be anywhere. Kasandra just had to find out where. Realizing her new role as part of the animal guard, Kasandra knew she would have to travel the world to find Crow and Vulture. She and her friends would stop them and save the world together. It would be great. They just needed a way to find out about the animals in danger. But how? Kasandra knew just the right person, but it required taking a few risks.

The next morning, Kasandra woke up early at five thirty. She planned to sneak Maria's phone from her room to call Shakira. Darling was sleeping over at Shakira's house, so the plan would work perfectly.

Kasandra carefully tiptoed into Maria's room, and saw the phone sitting on her desk. Kasandra swiftly grabbed it and brought it into her bedroom. She quickly dialed Shakira's number and then told her about her plans.

"You want to do what?" said Shakira puzzled.

"Shakira, I want to sneak high tech computers into my house. We could ask Miss Soul if it's okay if we use one of her computers that are in the storage cabinets," replied Kasandra.

Darling replied shortly after, "I guess that is a good plan. We have heard that those computers are cursed and haunted. So, no one would even want them. I bet Miss Soul is the last one who wants them."

"Bye, and see you at your house tomorrow," started Shakira, her voice getting louder, "and don't forget…. John will be there too!"

"Alright. Bye, and see you guys tomorrow!"

After hanging up, Kasandra sneaked into Maria's room, and placed the phone back to its original position. She returned to her own room and fell asleep reading more of Loriel Cortez's diary. She found it to be quite interesting.

The next morning, Kasandra went into Avó's room and helped her pack up her stuff. It was easy work. Avó paid Kasandra five dollars to pack up her camera and photo albums of them. Her favorite photograph was of her and her grandfather standing on the beach at sunset. It always made her tear up a little bit.

After helping Avó pack up, Kasandra took Avó's bags down to Dad's shiny new car. Dad recently purchased a Mercedes. America was treating them just fine. Dad made lots of money at his new job. He worked for a telephone company called AT&T.

Once down at the car, the family wished Avó a nice, safe trip home. Dad drove off with Avó to the airport. Maria and Mom went back inside, leaving Kasandra in the early morning daylight. Kasandra sat on the front deck, under the shelter of the overlapping roof. She sat on her red rocking chair, and soon saw a car pull up into the driveway. It was Darling's mother's car. Darling hopped out, kissed her mother goodbye, and came over to Kasandra sensing the earth around her, always aware of her surroundings although she could not see it with her eyes.

Darling approached Kasandra and said, "Hello! Shakira left an hour ago. She said she was going to unpack her things before she came over. So, she'll be here soon. What is it you wanted to tell me?"

Before Kasandra had the chance to answer, Darling continued, "Ohh! Yes. John will be coming over with Shakira."

"Yes. Come up to my room. It's pretty exciting," said Kasandra, leading the way inside. Darling followed Kasandra, and soon the two girls made it up to Kasandra's room. Kasandra took out the diary, and opened up to the page about the 'bad guys.'

Before the girls could begin reading, Kasandra heard a knock on the door. It was Shakira and John. Kasandra heard Maria say, "Come in. If you need Kasandra, she and her friend went upstairs."

"Thank you very much," Kasandra heard the muffled voice of Shakira say.

Soon after, they were all eagerly paging through the diary. Kasandra read part of it aloud to them, *"There are bad guys in the real world. They are brother and sister. Their names are Crow and Vulture."* That was all Kasandra read to them. Of course she left out a few things.

Kasandra talked to her friends about the plan to get the computers. They needed them if they were going to find some answers.

"So, we are going to ask for high tech computers from back in the day, and fight natural disasters that can ruin animal habitats?" asked Shakira, sounding nervous. No surprise there. Shakira was always nervous. Tests. Spelling bees. Soccer. Anything. It just was who she was. Kasandra loved her friend anyway. After all, she knew that everyone was different.

Once the group finalized their plans (and talked some more about what they were afraid of!), it was time for Shakira, Darling, and John to go home to enjoy the rest of the beautiful weekend. Kasandra said goodbye to her friends and sat on the lumpy sofa. She opened up her journal and started writing.

> *Dear journal,*
> *I hope you enjoyed watching my friends and I make our plans...*

She wrote all about her ideas and feelings. All she could do was confide in her journal and hope that their plan would turn out just fine the next day.

Chapter Twelve

Research

The next morning, the children walked into the library to ask Miss Soul about the computers. If their plan worked, they could get the computers without getting into any trouble. They all rode the bus to school today so they would get there earlier. They had extra time now.

As the group traveled down the hallway, the papers on the walls started to shake. The friends kept walking. Papers started falling off the walls. They continued to walk, until finally they reached the entrance to the library. They walked through the school library doors, and saw Miss Soul sitting at her desk, reading what appeared to be seven books. She seemed to be writing one too!

Miss Soul perked up from her pile of things, stood up and said, "Hello. What can I do for you today?"

"We would like to borrow those computers from fifteen years ago. They seem to be in good shape, they just need a little-" Kasandra sneezed mid-sentence, "dusting." She sneezed again.

"Well... If you really want them, you can take them," said Miss Soul, picking up her book and sitting back down. "They are in the back cabinet. Over to the left, Shakira. Not that way, John." Miss Soul appeared to drift off to sleep as her words fizzled to a whisper.

Darling opened up the closet door with a squeak. Inside were five computers, about the height of Julia and Jeremiah. Kasandra wondered how she was going to get these computers home. She looked around the library, and she saw a cart that was usually used by the janitor. *Perfect!* thought Kasandra as she crept along to the cart. To Kasandra's surprise, the cart was heavy. The worst part was the handle. The rust made Kasandra's hands ache. The journey to the closet itself was not hard. It was making the trip back. Finally, Kasandra got the cart over to her friends.

Now the friends just had to manage to get the computers onto the cart. Then out of the library. Then home. Easy. Or not. It all came down to these computers. Kasandra tried to lift one, but it was heavy. A little *too* heavy. Kasandra was upset now.

"Hey, guys? Can you help me lift this?" asked Kasandra, looking over at her friends.

"Sure," they replied in unison, hurrying over to Kasandra.

"On three," said Shakira.

"One... Two... Three!" Shakira counted loudly, but not loud enough to wake the sleeping librarian.

Finally, the youngsters lifted the computers and placed them safely onto the cart. They pushed the cart over to the library door when Kasandra said, "Thanks, Miss Soul. We really appreciate it."

"Why, you're quite welcome. What, what did I do again?" said Miss Soul.

Before Kasandra had the chance to reply, the librarian was already fast asleep again. This is what a day full of shelving books can do to a person!

Thank goodness I got mom to pick me up after school. Or I would have a lot of explaining to do with the bus driver, thought Kasandra, always trying to look on the bright side.

Later that day, Kasandra helped her mom load the computers into the car. Once they got home, Mom prepared dinner right away. They were having 'Cali Style Cauliflower' for dinner.

Once Kasandra finished eating her cauliflower, she heard the familiar knock of Shakira's hand hit the door. Kasandra ran over to the door and opened it. There was Shakira, Darling, and John standing in the doorway. Kasandra let them in and told them the computers were in the living room. The girls walked in and went right to work picking up the many computer pieces and bringing them upstairs. John, on the other hand, went up to the tight hideout, where he began searching for open outlets in the room.

They continued to work while John tested the outlets to be sure that they were all working. Kasandra felt it was the perfect time to give him a ring from her jewelry box, since he was now a part of their secret group too. She ran over to the box, and took out a ring with a yellow gem inside. It seemed like it would match the look of a parrot.

Kasandra walked over to John, put the ring in his hand and said, "I wanted to give this to you; so you feel like part of the group."

"Thanks a lot Kasandra!" John replied. He picked up the ring and studied it with great admiration. Kasandra looked down at her own ring. She smiled. It was *brilliant*.

With a grin on his face, John returned to his job of getting the computers up and running so the friends could begin their research. John slowly picked up the final cord and plugged it into the wall. As soon as he did this, the image of a woman appeared on the screen. She had curly black hair that puffed out to both sides. She looked down at the children.

Stunned, Kasandra asked, "Who are you?"

The strange woman pointed to a name tag that hung from the edge of her desk. It read '*Miss Caroline Kalisto.*'

"As you can see Miss Cortez, my name is Caroline Kalisto, but you will call me Miss Kalisto. Do you understand?"

"Yes," replied Kasandra, as she stared at the woman on the screen. *How did Miss Kalisto know my name?* she thought.

"How do you know my name, Miss Kalisto?" asked Kasandra. It was all she could think to say.

"I don't believe you read everything on my name tag," said Miss Kalisto, pointing down at her name tag once again. Under her name, it said, *'Secretary of Recruits 101.'*

"That makes more sense!" shouted Kasandra, as she jumped for joy.

"Now, settle down. Listen. I am supposed to tell you that you four have been recruited to join the Animal Guard. You will travel worldwide to save animals in every continent. But, you must use a specific object in order to travel using our advanced technology. It has to be something you all have," said Miss Kalisto.

Before Miss Kalisto could carry on with her speech, Darling exclaimed, "Our rings!"

"Yes. Those will do just fine. As I was saying," she looked over at Darling with a scowl, "Those objects will help you travel around the world in seconds. Once you get to the appropriate location, we will give you more information using these headphones." She was now holding what appeared to be the world's smallest headphones.

"But we don't have *those* headphones," said Shakira, crossing her arms over her chest.

"Yes you do," replied Miss Kalisto, who snapped her fingers once. All of a sudden, four pairs of headphones appeared on the ground behind John. It was like magic. It *was* magic. Or at least they thought it was. As it turns out, the organization has a very powerful teleportation system. Everyone grabbed a set of headphones, then moved towards the ginormous computers.

"I have a meeting in a few moments. Do you have any questions?" asked Miss Kalisto politely.

"Who are Crow and Vulture?" asked Kasandra, hoping for an honest answer.

Miss Kalisto stood still for a moment, like she was frozen in time. Then, she abruptly stated, "Well won't you look at the time! I better get going. Good luck agents!" The image of Miss Kalisto quickly disappeared.

"Why did you have to ask that Kasandra?" questioned Darling.

"I just had to. We need to know what we're going to be up against. Don't we?" replied Kasandra, slowly shifting her gaze away from the blank screen. The rest of the team quietly nodded and went back to work.

They spent the rest of the day, and into the night, researching the Animal Guard. They learned everything that they possibly could about animal defenses and places where they could possibly end up on a mission. It was harder than any one of them expected. Way harder.

Chapter Thirteen

The Key Detail

As the weeks passed, Kasandra waited for something exciting to happen. She waited. And waited some more. Still nothing happened. Until one morning Kasandra thought to herself, *Crow and Vulture are both types of birds, so maybe their spirit animals are birds!* She had to tell her friends. Kasandra thought about when she would get to see them again.

At that moment, Kasandra was busy wrapping a birthday present for Maria. Her older sister's birthday was coming up in just a few days. Kasandra bought Maria a beautiful bracelet that had several charms dangling from it. There were shiny gold charms, and flashy, silver ones too. Kasandra had spent almost fifty dollars on it.

Maria's friends from school are coming over to celebrate tomorrow. That means I could ask mom if my friends can come over too! Kasandra thought as she hid Maria's present under the bed. She ran downstairs as quickly as she could. Then, she burst into the kitchen to ask for her mother's permission.

"Gee, I guess that would do. It would be fair for you anyway. You just have to stay in your room with your friends. Do you understand?" said Mom, as she chopped up tomatoes and put them into a bowl.

"Yes, Mom. I will tell them to stay in my room with me. Thanks!" said Kasandra, running down the hall, and back up to her room. Once she reached her room, she took out her journal, and started writing.

The next day, Maria's friends began arriving around noon. They were going to play out in the yard. They were enjoying games like quoits and darts. Mom had told Kasandra that she was not allowed to go down to the yard for safety reasons. Kasandra was fine with that.

Shortly after a lunch of sandwiches and pizza with Maria and her friends, Kasandra's own friends arrived at her house. They went directly upstairs and into Kasandra's bedroom. Once they were safely in her room, the group started to discuss the recent events.

"So you figured something else out?" asked John in his casual voice.

"Yes," said Kasandra confidently.

"Man, you're good," replied John bashfully. He had never met a girl as amazing as Kasandra.

"So I was thinking yesterday about spirit animals, and then I realized that Crow and Vulture are both birds... which makes their spirit animals birds too! Maybe they can even fly!" said Kasandra.

"Nice thinking!" replied Shakira.

"Yes very good thinking, Kasandra," replied Darling right after Shakira.

"That also got me thinking. Do you remember when things would shake and fall to the ground?" said Kasandra, while the rest of the group recalled the times that it happened to them.

"Yeah," said the others.

"Crow and Vulture were spying on us! It makes so much sense know!" said Kasandra, whose smile was broader than ever.

"Do you hear something?" asked Shakira curiously. They all froze. Someone was out in the hallway, walking towards Kasandra and her friends.

"Quick! Into the closet! It could be Maria's friends!" shouted Kasandra as she rushed her friends into the closet.

"Hello? Is anybody here?" said the taunting voice. It continued, "Ugh! Where are they?" It took Kasandra a moment to recognize the irritating voice. It was Jessica. She must have come with Maria's boyfriend, Matthew.

Darling giggled at the sound of Jessica's frustration. Hearing Darling giggle, Jessica said, "Aha, the closet. Mom always says snoop around in other people's business when they aren't around." She slowly inched toward the door and began to turn the handle.

Kasandra looked down at her ring. It was glowing. She looked over at her friends' rings. They were glowing too. All of a sudden, the four of them disappeared in a puff of smoke.

"Gotcha!" Jessica shouted, whipping open the closet door. She looked around. No one was there. "Ugh!" she puffed in frustration, as she turned and continued snooping around in the rest of the room.

Chapter Fourteen

African Adventure

"Where are we?" asked Kasandra, as she brushed dirt off of her jeans. Ahead of her were zebras and gazelles grazing in the huge plain where they were standing.

"I believe we are in Africa," said Shakira. "Do you think this is our first mi-" Shakira was cut off by a gust of wind. The sky grew dark. Soon large droplets of rain started to fall onto the group around them. It was a storm.

"Quickly! Let's find a cave or something that will give us shelter!" shouted John, who was barely heard over the pouring rain.

The herds of animals began to run into a nearby cave for shelter. The animals ran quickly, cuddling close to their young. All of a sudden, Kasandra heard a squeal. It was a frightened squeal. Kasandra ran away from the group and towards the sound. Whatever it was, she was running towards the danger. She ran over the soggy plain, and through the long grass that was almost as tall as she was.

"Kasandra! Wait up! Where are you going?" shouted John.

"Well, let's follow her then!" shouted Shakira, loud enough that her friends could hear her over the booming thunder.

"What direction did she go? I can't head her footsteps in this storm!" shouted Darling, reminding her friends that she could not see.

"No time for geography. Darling! Take my hand!" shouted Shakira, grabbing Darling's hand and then running after John. They ran in the same direction as Kasandra. Soon, they saw what Kasandra saw. There, in the corner of a little alleyway between boulders was a young zebra. It was so young it nearly tripped over itself. In front of the zebra was an incredibly large, hairy hyena. The hyena moved closer to the zebra, causing the zebra to let out a high-pitched squeal. The hyena growled again. The zebra was trapped.

John looked over and saw Kasandra standing high on a rock trying to stay out of danger. She couldn't keep her eyes off of the scene before her. It was more dramatic than anything she had ever seen on TV or read about in books. Kasandra motioned for her team to follow her. Darling, John and Shakira made their way to were Kasandra stood. She anxiously said to them, "We need to save it! We'll need a distraction. I have an idea... I hope it works!"

"I'll be the distraction!" said Darling. "I can run faster than all of us. Shakira told me we came from the south where the other animals are taking shelter."

"Well then, you got the job!" said Kasandra.

"Nice thinking, Darling! The hyena won't go near that many animals," said John.

"Okay, we are going to count down from three. Then Darling you will run back. Once the hyena leaves, we will grab the zebra, and bring it back to its herd. Got it?" said Kasandra, wondering if her plan would really work.

"Got it!" replied the others in unison.

They got into their positions. Darling waited off to the right while John and Shakira stood behind Kasandra ready for her to take charge. "Three... two... one!" shouted Kasandra, looking over at John. John looked back.

"Caw Caw!" he shouted loud enough that the hyena could hear him. With that, Darling took off in a sprint. The hyena followed her with glee.

Kasandra, John and Shakira approached the young zebra and Kasandra gently picked it up. She spoke softly to the zebra. "Are you hungry, little one? You'll be back to your herd in no time." Looking up at her friends, Kasandra said, "Let's go."

The team proudly walked to the caves where Darling waited for them at the entrance. At the sound of their footsteps, Darling cried, "You made it! I was so worried!"

"*You* were worried? We were worried you could be gobbled up by that wild hyena!" exclaimed Shakira. Darling giggled, and started talking to them about what she did to stay busy while they were gone.

"You did the right thing, Kasandra," said John. "Now, do you know how to get us home?"

"I say we rub our rings," replied Kasandra thoughtfully.

"Shall we then?" asked Shakira.

"I say we do," said Darling.

The foursome got into a circle, and held their rings in the center. "Let's go home," stated Kasandra. They all rubbed their rings, and with that they disappeared into a cloud of smoke.

Chapter Fifteen

Back Home

Kasandra opened her eyes. She was back in her closet. "We did it!" she shouted, turning her head to make sure her friends were all there too.

"That was supercalifragilisticexpialidocious!" shouted Shakira, her eyes widening.

With a puzzled look on his face, John asked, "Why did you say that?"

Shakira came back quickly, "I said that because 'supercalifragilisticexpialidocious' is the word you say when you don't know what to say." She shrugged. "Well, at least that's what the dictionary says."

"Whatever," said John, rolling his eyes at Shakira.

"Can you two stop?" asked Kasandra politely.

"Yes," groaned Shakira and John.

"By the way, my mom said it would be okay for everyone to sleep over tonight," said Kasandra, quick to change the subject.

"I'm cool with it," said Darling.

"Me too," said Shakira. "Um, what about you John?" she continued, looking over at John.

"I guess I'll stay," he said with a smirk. Kasandra, Darling and Shakira laughed.

Once the giggling came to an end, Shakira said to the group, "We'll probably need to find a new hiding space before Jessica comes back. Let's get out of this closet!"

"Good idea! How about headquarters? Or the computer room?" suggested Kasandra.

The group made their way down the hall and through the small door that led to their private headquarters. As soon as they entered the room, the computer screen flickered on with a flash. Miss Kalisto's face came into view.

"Congratulations agents," said a smiling Miss Kalisto.

"Thank you, Miss Kalisto," replied Kasandra.

Miss Kalisto continued, "You successfully completed your first mission. However, Crow and Vulture are still out there. There is no telling when you will be called into action again. Now you need some rest. Goodbye agents."

"Goodbye," said Kasandra waving to Miss Kalisto.

As the screen blackened, Kasandra let out a long breath. Her lips slowly curled into a smile as she scanned the faces of her friends. With a newfound confidence, she declared, "Wow! We just did that!"